FAMILY ISSUES AND YOU™

DEALING WITH FAMILY RULES

ISOBEL TOWNE
AND LEA MACADAM

rosen publishing's
rosen
central®

NEW YORK

Published in 2016 by The Rosen Publishing Group, Inc.
29 East 21st Street, New York, NY 10010

Copyright © 2016 by The Rosen Publishing Group, Inc.

First Edition

Library of Congress CataloginginPublication Data

Towne, Isobel.
 Dealing with family rules / Isobel Towne and Lea MacAdam. — First edition.
    pages cm. — (Family issues and you)
 Includes index.
 ISBN 978-1-4994-3699-0 (library bound) — ISBN 978-1-4994-3697-6 (pbk.)
 — ISBN 978-1-4994-3698-3 (6-pack)
 1. Parent and child—Juvenile literature. 2. Children—Conduct of life—Juvenile
literature. 3. Families—Juvenile literature. I. MacAdam, Lea. II. Title.
 HQ755.85.T68 2016
 306.874—dc23
                                                                    2015020160

Manufactured in the United States of America

CONTENTS

INTRODUCTION

There are plenty of sayings and jokes about how rules are meant to be bent or broken, but these common expressions only show us how important rules really are. Try to think about someone who loves rules. Really, that number is pretty low. Even adults sometimes have a hard time following basic rules! And to be honest, few people truly enjoy enforcing rules. Rules might seem unnecessary and just something that our parents and other adults make up to challenge us or make our lives difficult. Maybe rules seem unfair or even dumb.

It doesn't matter whether we like them or not: Rules are here to stay. Just try to imagine how chaotic our lives would be without rules, laws, or regulations. Rules are around for a very good reason. No matter where you are—home, school, or anywhere out in public—if you want to get along with others you have to observe certain rules that make these situations more organized, logical, secure, and civilized.

As a kid, it seems like there's always another rule to remember. But don't forget, your parents or guardians are the ones who are responsible for raising you to become a good human being. They want to teach you how to live and share with others, and how to do what makes you happy as well as what makes sense. You probably won't always agree, but remember how much experience and knowledge your parents have. In this resource, you'll learn how to handle rules that don't make sense to you and how to approach your guardian or parent about it. And that's just one of the useful lessons you can learn as you read on.

Rules seem like a real drag, but they are there so we can learn how to live and share our lives happily with others.

CHAPTER ONE

THE NECESSITY OF CHORES

Just think about how much different life would be if no one in your family followed rules. What if everyone—even your parents—just did whatever they wanted all day, everyday? Very few people would choose to take out the garbage, vacuum the rugs, or weed the garden if they didn't have to. Most moms and dads really don't love to wash the dishes and clean the kitchen after they've been cooking or baking all afternoon.

If your parents do such things, it is not because they're fun but because if these tasks don't get done, your entire family will end up living in a messy and disorganized home. And though initially you might think this could be fun, eventually you'll want some order or cleanliness. To make your home function well, your mom or dad, or both, probably have a set of rules they obey to help them organize their time and get essential family chores done.

These kinds of rules are not necessarily written down. Many of them—such as buying food, paying bills, or emptying the garbage—have probably become a habit. Sometimes however, a parent might make a note of important "things to do" on a sticky yellow Post-It or on a calendar. Your parent does this not because he or she wants to make your life more difficult, but

If it wasn't for rules, few people would bother to do chores like taking out the garbage. And what a mess that would be.

because it is important for your entire family that certain things get done and that they get done on time.

BEING OLDER AND MORE RESPONSIBLE

When you were a little kid, your parents were in charge of doing most things around the house. This is normal. After all, they were bigger, smarter, and were quite simply better at folding laundry than you were. However, as you get older, you become capable of doing more. As you grow up, you become more independent. You also have more say in what goes on around your home. In return, you begin to have more responsibilities. Having responsibilities is part and parcel of becoming an adult. You don't want to reach the age of twenty-five and have your parents still doing everything for you. Your parents probably wouldn't be so thrilled by the idea either.

Being responsible means taking care of yourself and others—such as younger siblings—and your home. Your parents will probably put certain rules in place that will help you carry out your responsibilities.

JOBS AROUND THE HOUSE

A chore is a routine task or job you do around the house. Chores are often tiresome, and while they may not be anyone's favorite thing in the world, they have to be done.

In most families, your mom or dad or both do most of the chores. But as you and your siblings grow older, your parents will expect you to do chores as well. When you think about it, this is only fair, since you live with your parents and you don't even have to pay any rent. So even if you do have to shovel snow, dust, or babysit your little brothers, it's still a pretty good deal.

When Karissa's dad came home from work and dropped her heavy grocery bags on the kitchen floor, Karissa was in the den watching television.

"Karissa?" called Mr. Jacon. "Can you come help me with the groceries?"

"Hang on!" yelled Karissa. "I'm watching *Gotham*."

"Karissa, I need help now! And how come you haven't set the table?"

"Dad! I can't hear you! I'm watching TV!"

"And you didn't make pasta or heat up the stew either!"

"Dad! I'm missing a really good part!"

"Karissa!" Mr. Jacon came stomping into the den. "You know that Tuesdays and Thursdays I have to work late. We agreed that you'd set the table and have dinner ready when I got home. Didn't we agree on that?"

"Yeah… yeah…Can't we talk about this later?"

Mr. Jacon grabbed the remote and switched the television off.

"Hey, Dad!"

"Karissa, why didn't you do your chores?" "I was tired! I was at school all day!"

"Well guess what? I was at work all day and I'm tired, too. But I still had time to buy groceries for both of us. You live here, too. Is it too much to ask that you help out by setting the table, boiling some pasta, and heating up some stew?"

"Well, I wanted to watch *Gotham*!"

"Karissa, this household is more important than a TV show. If you do your chores first, I don't mind you watching TV. But we had an agreement."

"Alright, alright," sighed Karissa, getting to her feet. She went into the kitchen and began putting away the groceries.

WORKING FOR AN ALLOWANCE

Some kids get an allowance—a small sum of money— from their parents. Often the allowance is given in return for helping out around the house. Do you think that's a fair deal? Some parents think it is. They think that having an allowance teaches kids about responsibility.

"Mom," said Ianna, sauntering into the kitchen. "I think you should raise my allowance."

"Oh, really?" asked Mrs. Hahn, looking up from his bowl of granola. "And what will you do in return?"

"You mean I have to do more stuff around the house? Anna Caringi gets more money than I do and she doesn't have to do anything. Her family has a maid."

"Well that's nice for Anna and her family. Unfortunately, your dad and I don't make enough money to be able to afford a maid. And if I'm going to up your allowance, maybe you could help out a little more around the house. Is that so unreasonable?"

"I guess not," muttered Ianna. "What do I have to do?"

"Well," said Mrs. Hahn. "If you promise to water the houseplants and garden, mow the lawn, take out the compost, and take recycling to the box in the garage when the container is full, I'll give you an extra $10 a week. Deal?"

"Yeah, I guess."

"Do we need this in writing or will a simple handshake do it?"

"A simple handshake," said Ianna. "Oh, and can I have my raise right now?"

Doing household chores might not be your favorite thing, but it does give you some useful life experience that will help you become an independent adult. For example, Karissa already

If you ask your parents for a raise in your allowance, is it fair for them to ask you to do more work, like helping to weed the garden and pick veggies?

knows how to cook certain kinds of food. Ianna knows a little bit about gardening. Anna Caringi, with her live-in maid, probably doesn't know how to do any of these things. And later on in her life, when she lives on her own, she may wish that she did know how to do a few things around the house. And though it may be hard to believe, there are actually some people who find it relaxing to mow the lawn or weed the garden.

If you and your parents agree to certain rules, it is pretty lousy if you don't fulfill your obligations. How would you feel if your mom promised to drive you to and from soccer practice and then just decided that she had too much other stuff to do or that she was too tired to pick you up? You'd probably feel let down and even angry. If it happened more than once, you'd feel that your mom wasn't responsible and that you couldn't count on her.

Mrs. Hahn had to get up early and go to work. But she always left Ianna's allowance in an envelope on the kitchen table. One day, Ianna opened the envelope and found that half of his allowance was missing. Mr. Hahn was eating granola and doing homework for his night course at college.

"Hey! Mom shorted me!" exclaimed Ianna.

"What's the problem, Ianna?"

"Mom didn't pay me my whole allowance."

"Well, did you do all the chores you were supposed to do?" asked Mr. Hahn.

"Well..." Ianna hesitated. "I moved the lawn. I just didn't get around to watering plants or the garden yet."

"And have you seen that overflowing box of rcycling in the basement? And what about the compost?"

DOGS, CATS, AND OTHER PETS

Many kids have pets. Many other kids your age want pets. There is nothing like having a dog, cat, parrot, hedgehog, or even a bearded dragon of your own to play with and talk to. Of course, as you've probably heard a million times before, having a pet is a big responsibility. Regardless of whether the animal in question belongs to just you or to the whole family, there are going to be rules relating to that particular pet. And as full or part owner of Boots, Buster, or Max, it is up to you to see that the cat, dog, or turtle in question follows these rules.

Listen to your dad if he says you should not leave Bruiser the bulldog unattended in the yard because he'll trample the prize-winning tomato plants he's spent all summer growing. Don't let Bruiser out. If your mom objects to Prince the cat in her room because she's allergic and the cat sheds his lovely long fur all over the carpet and comforter, don't let Prince into your mom's room. He will make your mom sneeze and she'll be unhappy. Sometimes it seems like parents are just being difficult, are exaggerating, or are being mean to Bruiser and Prince. For everyone to live together peacefully in a home, everybody's likes and dislikes have to be respected. It might feel like you've told your brother a billion times not to let Munch, his guinea pig, run around in your bedroom since that time he ate the final draft of your research paper. How would you feel if he forgot about that rule and let Munch loose to munch his way through your college application papers?

"I've been busy, Dad!"

"That's too bad, Ianna. We're all busy and we get things done. I'm sure when you have time to get your chores done, your dad will give you the rest of your allowance."

FAMILY MATTERS

Housework is not the only kind of chore for which you might be responsible. And your mom or dad might not be the only ones who require you to pitch in at home. Your household might include other members, such as siblings or pets, who count on you, too.

If you're an older brother or sister, your parents might want you to take on some responsibilities by helping out with your younger siblings. Maybe your dad will ask you to pick up your little sister at the bus stop after school and walk her home safely. Maybe your mom will put you in charge of taking your little brother to his guitar lessons. If you're in charge, this means that you will be responsible for making sure your younger sibling stays safe by following rules that you already know. If you're crossing a street, it's up to you to remind your little sister to look both ways. If you're at home, in the kitchen, it's up to you to tell your little sister not to turn on the food processor even though the buttons are fun to push. Believe it or not, being responsible and following rules can make you feel good. Knowing that your family members can rely on you will give you a sense of maturity. After all, it's good to be trustworthy.

If you're a younger brother or sister, your parents might want your older siblings to help take care of you. Although your parents make up the rules in your house, when they aren't around it is up to your older brother or sister to make sure that the normal household rules are being followed. Though it may be tempting,

Anyone with younger siblings might be asked to help take care of them. For example, you might be asked to help teach your sister how to do dishes.

don't make his or her life miserable by taking advantage of the fact that your parents aren't home. At the same time, your older siblings shouldn't make your life miserable by inventing rules of their own that you all know your parents wouldn't approve of.

CHAPTER TWO

FINALLY, FREE TIME

At last, the dishes are washed and put away, the dog has been walked, you packed lunches for you and your brother for school the next day, and finished your own homework. Now you're allowed some time to rest, relax, or play. No matter what you want to call it, free time or downtime is important, too.

Of course, rules and regulations don't stop just because your chores are done. There is a big difference between kicking back safely and smartly and kicking back stupidly. Also, when you're relaxing at home, you have to remember that you're not the only one in your house. Your parents and siblings might have other things they want to do, such as rest, do homework, stream live concerts on the computer, or take time for a video chat with a friend who moved far away. You have to re-

Even free time sometimes needs rules. For example, it's polite to check with your family when you want to have friends over and belt out some karaoke tunes.

spect what they want to do just as they should respect what you want to do. The only problem is that sometimes not everybody can do what they want at the same time in the same house. If there are no household rules established, conflicts are bound to come up.

SCREEN TIME

Most kids your age like to watch a little bit of TV from time to time. There is nothing wrong with that. There are some really good shows out there that are intelligent and interesting and entertaining. Unfortunately, there are even more programs that are dumb, boring, and a big waste of time. Some people can get easily addicted to television. It can happen before you're aware of it. Just sit back in a chair and channel surf or lose all track of time streaming shows on the computer. It takes less effort than reading a book, going for a hike, or playing a game of basketball with your friends.

If your parents feel that you are spending too much time in front of the television set or computer screen, they could have a point. Television is good in small doses. Smartphones are brilliant little gadgets that put all kinds of access right in our pockets. There are plenty of other activities to take advantage of. Since your parents are in charge of your education and upbringing, they certainly have the right to set limits on how many hours you spend in front of the television, playing video games, or on the computer or phone. Not only should they have a say in how much you watch, but what you watch as well. There is a lot of violence, sex, and sheer stupidity out there, no matter how it is accessed. Not all of it is meant to be watched by someone your age. Just as there are age limits placed on drinking in a bar or

It's easy to lose track of time when you're watching a great television show. Some parents ask their kids to limit their TV time or other "screen time."

getting into an R-rated movie, your parents might want to place limits on the kinds of TV shows you watch, whether they're on television or the computer.

Jamal's parents thought his screen time was getting out of hand. In the last six months, he had put on weight just from sitting in front of the television or computer, even though he had not changed his eating habits. He was also not getting much homework done. His grades on his last report card had been alarming.

"Jamal, your excessive TV watching and online gaming is becoming a problem," his father said to him. "Your mother and I have talked it over and we want you to make up a list of the television shows you'd like to watch and the games you want to play every week. We want to see the times the shows are on and we're going to research them to make sure they are appropriate for you to be watching. The same goes for the games you're playing. We'll set a time limit for the amount of screen time you're allowed each week. And each day before you turn on the set or play games, you'll have to show either your mother or me your homework. If it's not done, no TV or video games."

Jamal was unhappy with this agreement. It was going to be really hard to narrow down all those great programs and games. But he could see his dad's point of view. He definitely didn't want to risk repeating eighth grade.

CELL PHONES AND LANDLINES

Just as addictive as flicking on the television is talking on the phone. A kid who eats, breathes, and lives on the phone is one of the biggest nightmares a parent can have. Whether it's tying up the line for hours, racking up big phone or data bills, or getting infinite phone calls and text messages from friends late at night or in the middle of meals, kids and phones sometimes go together too well for their own (and everybody else's) good.

Of course you're going to want to chat with friends, set up meetings, and catch up on the day's gossip, but you have to

Parents might set down some rules if they feel their kids are using the phone too much or using up too much of the family's data plan.

remember that others share your house. This means that they share the phone, too. Unless you have call-waiting, or everyone has their own cell phone, it's really infuriating if your dad is trying to call to say he is stuck in traffic and is going to be hours late for dinner and he can't get through because you're telling your friend Suzanne how cute Jonathan is. It could even be dangerous if it turns out your dad was in an accident. And what if you have other siblings who like to chat as much as you do? Even if some of you have your own cell phones, your house will be full of kids fighting for who gets the phone next and for how long.

If your parents feel that you, and perhaps your other siblings, are spending too much time on the phone, they will probably set down some rules. These could range from setting up specific times when you can make calls—such as after dinner, after having done your homework, and before your bedtime—to how much time each call should last (an hour is pushing it). Some parents might decide to let you have your own private cell phone. If they are feeling really generous, they might even pay for it. Of course, if you feel your parents are being too strict and are not letting you talk at all on the phone, you can suggest having your own phone. You can even offer to pay half or all of the charges and agree to keep track of your minutes and data so you don't go over and rack up charges. That will show them how responsible you can be.

COMPUTER TIME

Right up there with television and telephones is the Internet. As more kids have access to computers and learn how to surf the Net, more cyberaddicts are being born every day. Like television, the Internet can be a great source of both information and entertainment. It also contains a lot of violent and sexual material

SNACK TIME

Coming home after school and enjoying a homemade cookie and a glass of milk is a classic of a North American childhood. Unfortunately, the image is more fiction than fact. The fact is many kids come home from school and want to relax. And all too frequently, snacking is associated with relaxing. Often, when kids come home from school, they plop themselves in front of the television and grab a bag of chips. Then, before they know it, they have demolished the whole bag. According to the Centers for Disease Control (CDC), "In 2012, more than one third of children and adolescents were overweight or obese." In the United States, about half of all adults are overweight, according to the National Childhood Obesity Foundation. And in Canada, according to the Childhood Obesity Foundation of Canada, that number is about 59. And this is not because of gland problems. It's because of eating poorly and eating too much.

Most households have rules about what snacks are acceptable between meals. Eating too much of any food could ruin your appetite for the next meal.

Parents usually have rules about what their kids should and shouldn't eat. And if you look at the statistics, you can see why it is important to have such rules in place. Junk food should be limited. So should eating between meals. This is because eating between meals ruins your appetite. It can become a bad habit that leads to excessive weight gain. Not to mention that it's rude if someone goes to the trouble of preparing a nice dinner, but beforehand you head out for some milkshakes and French fries.

that is not put out there for kids your age. Like a telephone, the Internet is a great way to communicate with your friends and to find information. However, endless surfing can also tie up the computer—especially if more than one of you needs to use it for school—and distract you from other things that you need to do (remember homework?). Because of these downsides to the Internet, it makes sense that your parents try to set some rules about how and when you log on.

You should also be aware that though it might be fun to meet new friends on social media websites like Facebook or chat apps, you do have to be cautious in your communications, especially in terms of giving out personal information. Your parents may come up with strict rules in terms of your Internet and e-mail communications. And however unfair this may seem (after all, it is exciting to meet new people online), there have been many cases where kids your age have met up with their new supposed friends, only to find themselves in dangerous situations. So when your parents say that they don't want you to meet up with your cyberfriend unless you are accompanied by an adult, listen up. They may be saving you from trouble.

STAYING SAFE AROUND THE HOUSE

In many ways, hanging out and playing at home is safer than playing in a park or in the streets. At home you don't have to worry about cars and traffic, muggers, bullies, and attacking pit bulls. Your home is safe and familiar and there is usually someone older around whom you can run to if anything serious should happen.

However, certain types of accidents can happen when you're horsing around at home. And often, your parents will set down a few rules that, even though they might seem strict, are mostly about keeping you, your family, and your home safe.

Plenty of safety rules are common sense and everyone knows them. By a certain age kids probably know not to stick anything into electrical sockets or play around with stoves or matches. Most kids understand they should not open the door to someone unless they have their parents' permission to let that person come into their home.

Some parents keep one or more guns in the house. Their rules about not touching these weapons without their permission and supervision are some of the most important household rules to follow. Way too many kids shoot themselves, their friends, or their siblings by accident. According to the Centers for Disease Control (CDC), 1,337 kids under the age of eighteen died as a result of gunshot wounds in 2010. With statistics like that, every kid should realize how crucial gun safety is and to follow the house rules without question.

CHAPTER THREE

OUT AND ABOUT

Whether you live with one or more parents, your grand-parents, or other guardian, it's important to accept that they are responsible for deciding what the house rules will be. The older you get, the more responsibilities you have, but at the same time you get more independence and freedom to do what you want. For most teens this means they spend more time outside their home, such as at school functions, clubs, or just chilling out with friends at their houses, at malls, or outside at parks. Many teens hang out in restaurants, at the movies, or at parties when the weekend rolls around.

Of course, your parents aren't going to tag along to supervise you. And if you're at school or at a friend's house, your parents aren't the ones making the rules. Your parents will expect you to do what is right based on the rules you have

As kids get older, their parents give them more freedom and responsibilities. Following their rules when you're out at the mall will show them you can be trusted.

learned at home. If they give you permission to do things outside the house, it is because your parents trust you and believe that you are responsible enough to make independent decisions and follow other rules. Every time you break a rule—whether at home, at school, in a store, or at a friend's house—you will be convincing your parents (and others) that you are not responsible enough to be independent. Breaking rules can lead to your parents setting down new, stricter rules. It is up to you to prove that you can follow rules. This is the best way of convincing your parents to ease up on strict limits and give you more freedom.

STAYING SAFE

Parents worry about their kids' safety. They don't want you running around day and night doing whatever you want and possibly getting into trouble. You probably don't want that either. Everybody needs boundaries. In fact, it is proven that kids whose parents set no rules or limits are unhappy. They sometimes think that their parents don't care about them. Often, kids get into trouble because they don't know how to place limits on their own behavior.

Because they want you to be safe, your parents might establish certain rules such as curfews or calling home if you think you'll be late for dinner. Your parents want you to be independent. But learning how to deal with independence takes time.

Robin was excited when she was invited to Becca's party. She only hoped her mom would let her go. Ever since Robin's stepdad had left, her mom had been really down on relationships. Especially when she had been drinking.

Sure enough, when Robin asked permission, her

BAD BEHAVIORS

Smoking, drinking, and drugs are nasty habits. All can be dangerous, expensive, and highly addictive, especially if you get started at a young age, when you have less experience and less resistance. Furthermore, underage drinking and use of drugs are illegal. If your parents have rules forbidding you to drink and do drugs, they are not being unfair or super strict. They are only abiding by the rules of society, which sees these activities as criminal.

In terms of smoking, parents are concerned with your health. It is scientifically proven that smoking is one of the leading causes of death in the United States. If your parents get on your case because they smell cigarette smoke on your clothes, know that they are not just trying to boss you around. Chances are they care about you living a full and healthy life.

Some parents don't want their kids going places where they feel drugs and alcohol will be around. Sometimes their worries are valid, sometimes not. As you probably know, drugs and alcohol are all over the place—at school, in the streets—but you can't just spend your life hiding out at home. If your parents don't want you drinking or taking drugs, prove that you are reliable and trustworthy. Even if you go to a party where you think some kids might be drinking or smoking, don't get pressured into joining in if you know that it's going against your parents' rules. Usually, if your parents know that they can rely on you, they'll ease up on their worrying and strictness. However, if you come home sloshed one night or reeking of pot, how good will your chances be of getting permission to go out the next time?

mom asked if there would be boys there.

"Probably," murmured Robin.

"What do you mean 'probably'?" demanded Mrs. Hymes, taking a sip of bourbon. "Yes or no?"

"Yes," said Robin.

"You're too young to be hanging out with boys at parties. Boys are bad news. Especially at parties where drugs and drinking are involved."

"Look, Mom," said Robin. "Becca's mom is going to be at home. And there's not going to be any drinking or drugs. If it makes you feel better, I'll give you Mrs. Ritchie's number and you can call her. And if you let me go, I promise to be home by midnight."

"Midnight! Are you crazy?" exclaimed Mrs. Hymes. "If I let you go, you better be home by 10:00."

"How about 11:00?" tried Robin.

"Alright, alright, alright," conceded Mrs. Hymes. "But if you're more than ten minutes late, that's the last party you'll ever go to."

"BE HOME BY ..."

Many parents give their kids curfews. You might think it unfair that you have to be home from the movies or hanging out with friends at 10:00 p.m. when your best friend gets to stay out until 11:00. But different parents have different rules. If you think your parents are being unfair, talk to them. Ask them if they have specific reasons why you should be home at 10:00 and not 11:00. If they don't have

If you want permission to stay out later at night, consider negotiating an agreement that makes everyone happy. Some kids even print out a contract they and their parents sign.

specific reasons, offer an alternative curfew. Or you can try to negotiate.

Rune wanted to go and see the Avett Brothers in concert. But the concert wouldn't be over until 11:00 p.m. and Rune's curfew was 10:00.

"Aw come on, Dad," Rune pleaded with his father.

"Rune, the last time I let you stay out until 11:30, you didn't show up until nearly midnight."

"Yeah, I know. I lost track of time."

"You have a cell phone."

"Listen," said Rune to his dad. "Why don't you give me a trial 11:30 curfew? Just for two weeks. If I'm late once, we automatically go back to 10:00. No griping. I'll even draw up a contract on the computer to make it all official."

"Yeah, okay," grumbled Rune's dad. "I guess if it's in writing, I'll be safe."

PUNCTUALITY

Most people are late from time to time. Some people make a bad habit of it. Out there in the real world, lateness can be a problem. Adults who are not punctual for work can get fired. Students who are late for school too often can get suspended.

Obviously if you are late in getting home from a play or skating with your friends, your parents aren't going to fire you or suspend you. However, if they are sitting around the dinner table waiting for you while your mom's homemade macaroni and cheese dish gets cold, they are not going to be pleased.

Everyone is late now and then, but it's important not to make it a habit. If someone is always late for dinner, the family is not happy waiting.

When you know your parents expect you to be home at a specific time, make sure you're on time. Some people set an alarm on their watch or phone to remind them when it's time to leave or check in at home. If you realize there's no way you're going to make it home in time, call or send a text message as soon as you can. Most parents will appreciate it if you are considerate enough to take a few minutes and let them know that the concert ran long with extra encores or that you dropped by Azurah's apartment to meet her new parakeet.

CHAPTER FOUR

HARMONY AT HOME

There's no way around it. We all need rules if we are going to get along with one another. Think about how different school would be if there weren't rules about taking turns speaking up in class by raising your hand, using cell phones during lessons, or skipping class. Rules are just as important at home. But rules are a two-way street. Guardians and parents can make rules for their homes, but you have a say sometimes, too. Kids and teens are just as much a part of the household as the parents are!

A PLACE OF ONE'S OWN

Everybody needs some time alone in a space that is his or her own. This is really important in a house or apartment where many people live together in close quarters.

From time to time, your parents or siblings will want to be by themselves in their rooms. If they have rules about you not barging in without knocking, not interrupting while they are talking on the phone, or letting them sleep until after 10:00 a.m. on a Sunday morning, then respect their rules and wishes. Similarly, don't read your little sister's diary, rifle through your brother's backpack, or snoop on anyone's cell phone or private e-mail.

33

Without their permission, you are invading their privacy. Privacy is a two-way street. As you start to move up in your teen years, part of your new independence will include wanting some privacy at home. To make sure that your family respects your privacy, you might want to establish some rules, too. Although you can't ban your parents and siblings from your room, you can ask them not to enter without knocking first if the door is closed. You can also ask them not to go through your private things, not to read your e-mail, and not to listen in on your phone calls. Some parents have trouble accepting their kids' growing independence. Others might be snoopy or distrustful. Unless you have given them good reason to have these attitudes, they have no right to break your rules of privacy. Unfortunately, short of talking to them and even getting angry, there isn't much you can do about nosy parents.

Everyone has his or her personal space and property that is for him or her alone. So follow these rules and be considerate about personal property like diaries.

FASHION FLEXIBILITY

Of course, some parents might be inflexible or traditional. They might object to a son who wears really baggy cargo pants or a daughter who wears a very mini miniskirt. Naturally, different clothes are suitable for different occasions. But what your parents might see as sloppy, you might view as cool. If you think your parents are being uptight, try to explain your point of view. If they persist and forbid you to wear the things you like, try negotiating. Say you won't wear these clothes to school or when you go out as a family, but that you'd like to wear them on casual occasions when you go out with your friends or on weekends.

You might not agree with your mom about appropriate school clothes. It helps if you reasonably explain why you think you should be able to wear a certain style.

GOOD MANNERS

It seems as if adults are always complaining about kids not being polite. They like to talk about how "back in my day" nobody swore and everybody said "Please, ma'am" and "Thank you, sir." Well, for better or for worse, times have changed. And so have manners and the use of language. In general, American society has become more laid-back and casual. And certain slang expressions have become the norm. Nonetheless, your parents might expect certain forms of politeness from you, both in and outside of your home. They want you to be well respected, well educated, and well liked. Knowing how to act appropriately in many different situations is part of this.

Sometimes, your parents might have very definite ideas about how they want you to behave if their friends come over, if you go visit some relatives, or if an important person calls on the telephone. You might be familiar with some of these rules: "Don't swear," "Don't pick your nose," "Don't talk with your mouth full," "Don't leave someone's house without saying 'thank you' and 'good-bye,'" "Don't fight with your little brother in public," "Keep your voice down," "Don't leave the table before everybody has finished eating," "Don't eat with your hands," "Don't stick your finger in your ear," and that's just a small sample. Parents like you to be polite because not only do your good manners make you look good, it makes them look good as parents as well.

Of course, if you're expected to act in a mature and in-control adult manner, your parents should be willing to do the same. They shouldn't yell at you in public. They shouldn't swear, pick their noses, or leave the table before everybody has finished eating either. If you're expected to speak nicely and politely to their friends on the phone or in the house, then your parents

These days it's fine to have casual manners sometimes, but your parents might want you to follow certain rules at the dinner table or when guests are visiting.

should always treat your friends with the same consideration and respect.

KEEPING CLEAN

Aside from politeness, parents also seem to go on a great deal about cleanliness. And you have to admit that they might just have a point. Even the most well-mannered, courteous, charming ten- or twelve-year-old will have a hard time making a good impression if his hair is uncombed, his jeans have big holes, his elbows are dirty, his breath stinks, and his room looks like a pigsty. If you are not measuring up to your parents' standards in the neat-and-tidy category, they might feel obliged to set down some rules. Some of the most common include "Wash your hands before coming to the table," "Don't go out wearing dirty, wrinkly, or ripped clothes," "Change your socks and underwear every day," "Make your bed," "Clean up your room," "Hang up your clothes," "Wash out the bathtub," "Don't throw stuff on

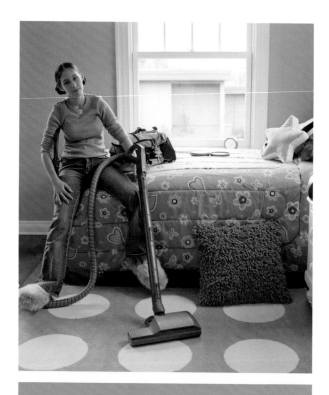

Most parents have ideas and rules about how clean your room should be. They might have a rule about how often you need to vacuum your carpet.

the floor," and "Rinse your dishes." Once again, these are only a few examples.

You might get tired of their nagging, but nobody wants to live in a dirty or messy house. More important, nobody wants to clean up somebody else's dirt and mess. And shutting the door to your bedroom and telling your parents to keep out if they don't want to see any tornado zones is not a useful solution. Being neat and clean is just as important as being courteous and respectful. Others base their opinions of you—and of your parents—on how you act.

When both sides feel satisfied that they are both giving and receiving, a compromise is a success. By just remembering this one simple rule, relationships with all kinds of people will go a lot more smoothly.

GLOSSARY

addiction The condition of being dependent on a substance such as drugs or alcohol.

allowance The giving of a fixed sum of money.

apps Computer programs or software designed to carry out specific functions; short for applications.

bearded dragon A lizard that has a beardlike pouch with spines on its throat; also called a bearded lizard.

chores Tasks or jobs that are done around the home.

compost Organic or vegetable matter that is decayed and made into fertilizer.

compromise When two parties each give something up to resolve their differences.

conflict A disagreement or fight.

curfew A set hour to be at home at night.

cyberaddict One who becomes addicted to using computers or related electronics.

data A measure of information used on a cellphone or computer, such as for Internet, e-mail, and apps.

enforce To carry out.

essential Something that is necessary.

guardian Someone, usually an adult, who is legally responsible for a minor, or young person, or individual who is otherwise unable to care for him- or herself.

landline A conventional telephone, which connects users by cables laid across land, either by poles or underground.

maturity Being fully grown, physically as well as mentally and emotionally.

negotiate To bargain with someone in order to reach an agreement.

punctual Occurring or happening at an appropriate or agreed upon time.

valid Something that is worthwhile or just.

FOR MORE INFORMATION

Adolescent and School Health
Centers for Disease Control and Prevention
4770 Buford Hwy, NE
MS K-29
Atlanta, GA 30341
(800) CDC-INFO (800-232-4636)
Website: http://www.cdc.gov/healthyyouth/index.htm
This division of the CDC is geared toward healthy young peo-
    ple and teens, including dealing with drugs and alcohol and
    links to BAM! Body and Mind, as well as multimedia options.

Big Brothers Big Sisters of America
National Office
2202 N. Westshore Blvd, Suite 455,
Tampa, FL 33607
(813) 720-8778
E-mail: national@bbbs.org
Website: http://www.bbbs.org
Big Brothers Big Sisters has been helping children thrive for
    more than one hundred years. They are the nation's largest
    mentoring network, offering support for children to succeed
    in life.

Big Brothers Big Sisters of Canada
3228 South Service Road, Suite 112E
Burlington, ON L7N 3H8
Canada
(800) 263-9133
Website: http://www.bigbrothersbigsisters.ca
"We commit to Canada's young people that we will be leaders
    in providing them with the highest quality, volunteer based
    mentoring programs."

Centers for Disease Control and Prevention
1600 Clifton Road
Atlanta, GA 30329-4027 USA
(800) CDC-INFO (800-232-4636)
Website: http://www.cdc.gov
In addition to copious information about healthy living, the Centers for Disease Control and Prevention offers tips for parenting and developing healthy household rules.

Childhood Obesity Foundation
771A – 2635 Laurel Street
Robert H.N. Ho Research Centre
VGH Hospital Campus
Vancouver, BC V5Z 1M9
Canada
Children and families can get support and information about healthy living and eating for everyone in the family.

Families Anonymous
701 Lee St., Suite 670
Des Plaines, IL 60016
(800) 736-9805
(847) 294-5877
Website: http://www.familiesanonymous.org
This twelve-step program offers support to families and friends of those who suffer with addictions to drugs, alcohol, and other behavioral issues.

Healthy Families BC
c/o Healthy Living Branch
4000 Seymour Place
Victoria, BC V8W 4S8

Canada
E-mail: healthyfamiliesbc@gov.bc.ca.
Website: https://www.healthyfamiliesbc.ca
The Healthy Families BC website encourages healthy living
for families by "focusing on four key areas: healthy eating,
healthy lifestyles, resources for parents, and fostering healthy
communities."

Women's and Children's Health Network
6 Gillingham Road
Elizabeth, South Australia 5113
Website: http://www.cyh.com
The Women's and Children's Health Network offers young people information about healthy living. This website includes
useful tips to help teens communicate effectively with their
parents, especially when there is conflict.

WEBSITES

Because of the changing nature of Internet links, Rosen Publishing has developed an online list of websites related to the sub-
ject of this book. This site is updated regularly. Please use this
link to access the list:

http://www.rosenlinks.com/FIY/Rules

FOR FURTHER READING

Bachel, Beverly K. *What Do You Really Want? How to Set a Goal and Go for It!* Paradise, CA: Paw Prints Press, 2008. Kindle ed.

Berry, Joy. *Every Kid's Guide to Family Rules and Responsibilities* (Living Skills Book 7). Wheaton, IL: Watkins Publishing House, 2013. Kindle ed.

Berry, Joy. *Every Kid's Guide to Understanding Parents* (Living Skills Book 24). Wheaton, IL: Watkins Publishing House, 2013. Kindle ed.

Carlson, Richard. *Don't Sweat the Small Stuff for Teens: Simple Ways to Keep Your Cool in Stressful Times.* New York, NY: Hyperion, 2012. eBook.

Carlson, Richard. *Don't Sweat the Small Stuff with Your Family: Simple Ways to Keep Daily Responsibilities and Household Chaos from Taking Over Your Life.* New York, NY: Hyperion, 2013. eBook.

Corwin, Donna G. *The Tween Years.* Lincolnwood, IL: Contemporary Books, 1998.

Covey, Stephen R. *The 7 Habits of Highly Effective Families: Building a Beautiful Family Culture in a Turbulent World.* New York, NY: St. Martin's Press, 2010.

Covey, Sean *The 7 Habits of Highly Effective Teens.* New York, NY: Simon and Schuster, 2014.

Covey, Sean. *The 7 Habits of Highly Effective Teens Personal Workbook.* New York, NY: Simon and Schuster, 2014.

Keltner, Nancy, ed. *If You Print This, Please Don't Use My Name: Questions from Teens and Their Parents About Things that Matter.* Norwich, VT: Terra Nova Press, 1992.

Kimball, Gayle. *The Teen Trip: The Complete Resource Guide.* Chico, CA: Equality Press, 1996.

McGraw, Jay. *Life Strategies For Teens* (Life Strategies Series). New York, NY: Touchstone, 2014. eBook.

Mosatche, Harriet S., and Karen Unger. *Too Old for This, Too Young for That*. Minneapolis, MN: Free Spirit Publishing, 2000.

Packer, Alex J. *Bringing Up Parents: The Teenager's Handbook*. Minneapolis, MN: Free Spirit Publishing, 1992.

Pollack, William S., and Todd Shuster. *Real Boys' Voices*. New York, NY: Random House, 2000.

Shipp, Josh. *The Teen's Guide to World Domination: Advice on Life, Liberty, and the Pursuit of Awesomeness*. New York, NY: St. Martin's Griffin, 2013. Kindle ed.

INDEX

ABOUT THE AUTHORS

Isobel Towne is an author and editor specializing in science and philosophy. She lives on the coast of northern Maine with her family, where they all try to take part in making fair family rules.

Lea MacAdam grew up in Topeka, Kansas, before moving to New York City. She works as a writer and photographer and is single-handedly raising two (mostly) rule-abiding children.

PHOTO CREDITS

Cover (figure) rnl/Shutterstock.com; cover (background), p. 1 clockwise from top left Monkey Business Images/Shutterstock.com, Sergey Kamshylin/Shutterstock.com, Kotin/Shutterstock.com, Jaren Jai Wicklund/Shutterstock.com; p. 3 sezer66/Shutterstock.com; pp. 4-5 Jupiterimages/Creatas/Thinkstock; pp. 6, 16 (top), 25 (top), 33 Monkey Business Images/Shutterstock.com; p. 7 Barry Austin Photography/Iconica/Getty Images; p. 11 Francesca Yorke/Photolibrary/Getty Images; pp. 15, 22 Fuse/Thinkstock; p. 16 Stockbyte/Thinkstock; p. 18 Geo Martinez/Shutterstock.com; p. 20 arek_malang/Shutterstock.com; p. 25 Minerva Studio/Shutterstock.com; pp. 28-29 © iStockphoto.com/pixdeluxe; p. 31 © iStockphoto.com/Christopher Futcher; p. 34 © iStockphoto.com/art-siberia; p. 35 Syda Productions/Shutterstock.com; p. 37 Asia Images Group/Getty Images; p. 38 Ryan McVay/Photodisc/Thinkstock; cover and interior pages patterns and textures Irina_QQQ/Shutterstock.com, ilolab/Shutterstock.com, Cluckv/Shutterstock.com, phyZick/Shutterstock.com; back cover Anna-Julia/Shutterstock.com

Designer: Michael Moy; Editor: Heather Moore Niver; Photo Researcher: Sherri Jackson